As The Blade Cuts

written by Eric Kapitan

Copyright © 2016 by Eric Kapitan
All rights reserved. This book or any portion thereof may not be reproduced or used in any manner whatsoever without the express written permission of the publisher except for the use of brief quotations in a book review.

This is a work of fiction. Names, characters, businesses, places, events and incidents are either the products of the author's imagination or used in a fictitious manner. Any resemblance to actual persons, living or dead, or actual events is purely coincidental

ISBN-13: 978-1519198723
ISBN-10: 1519198728

Acknowledgments

A special thank-you to David Sharp and Coleen Parker for their excellent feedback and editing suggestions. I would also like to thank my grandmother, Kathy Stone, for taking the time to read and encourage my crazy writing.

Thank you to anyone who buys and reads this book. I am very grateful for your support. I hope you enjoy reading As The Blade Cuts as much as I enjoyed writing it.

Please be sure to check out Beneath the Underground (http://beneaththeunderground.com/) a great website that features news, reviews, and all cool stuff related to the underground world of horror.

Contents

As the Blade Cuts...1
Cut Me Open..3
The Operation..5
Ain't It Great to Be Dead?...6
March of the Bloody Dead...8
Halloween Night II: The Sacrifice..10
Frozen Flesh...12
Foreign World...14
Inner Demons...16
Vampires Are Monsters..18
Creature in the Swamp...19
Whore Killin' (Yeah, You Be Offended!)..............................20
You Go When You Gotta Go..22
When It Came..24
The Cornfield...26
The Modern Monster..28
His Body Still Moves...30
The Chair...32
Hunger and Sex..33
The Officer..35
The Night Rage Filled the Air...38
The Road..40
One for the Fire...42
The Door at the End of the Hall..44
The Horse...45
My Darling...47
He Never Let Go..48
Carla and Craig..50
Blood Red..52
Today Is My Day...53
The Collection...55
Perfection..57
Food for the Maggots..59
Feast for the Crabs..61
Heat Wave...62
Blood Flow..64

Home Invasion	65
Dinnertime	66
The Blackest Day	68
Merry Fucking Christmas	70

Cover designed by Adam Beckley
https://www.facebook.com/adambeckleyartist

Bloodthristy font created by Jonathan Harris
http://tattoowoo.com/

This book is dedicated to my family. They have always supported my crazy insane ideas, and I love them for it.

As The Blade Cuts

Eric Kapitan

As the Blade Cuts

I push you on the bed,
handcuff your hands to the post.

Your top comes off as you cry.
The bra comes next.

I admire the canvas your body provides.
My hands caress the skin,
ready to create my masterpiece.

Carefully laying out my tools of the trade.
Beautiful light reflects off the tip of the blade.
Running my fingers along each one.

You breathe heavy as the blade slides through.
Your flesh opens like a flower in bloom.

Glowing red flows,
running down your soft skin.
My tongue licks it away.
The taste of iron pollutes my senses.

Your screams bounce off the walls,
drowning out my words.
My lips move.
You can't hear the sound.

Hours pass as I wipe sweat from my brow.
You vomit from the pain
as my blade travels your skin.

As The Blade Cuts

Pictures fall as my camera flashes—
images to remember.
Purple spots float in your sight.

I make love to you—
a lifeless doll lost in your mind.

My vision brought to life—
a portrait of myself
clashing with your beauty.
Now you're ugly like me.

Eric Kapitan

Cut Me Open

Tie me to the table.
I know you fear me.
Cut me wide open.
Take a look inside.

Every organ is there,
even a heart,
which you thought I never had.
You wash the blood off your hands.
I've already infected you.

Take a saw to my head.
Look inside my brain.
You won't like what you see.

The dreams I dreamed,
the thoughts I thought—
they stay with you,
images burned in your head.

Study my mind for days.
Try to find a pattern,
a reason.
Soon you will see
none exists,
no explanation.

The things that happened,
the people I hurt—
I loved every minute.

As The Blade Cuts

So cut me open.
Feel my warm blood on your hands.

Be scared when you see the truth.
I'm simply a man like you.

Eric Kapitan

The Operation

White light fills my eyes.
The vision fades in.
Loud machines echo.

People in white huddle over me,
unaware that I'm awake.
I try to move, but my muscles refuse.
I try to speak, but I can't form words.

I see a glimpse of silver—
a sharp blade.
It glimmers in the light.

The blade pierces my chest and belly.
The tip of it forms a Y in my skin.
The pain burns hot.
I put all my thoughts and energy into moving—
anything to stop this torture.
Nothing happens.

My body asleep.
Awake in my mind.
Eyeballs twitch.
Slowly, my chest is pulled apart.

As The Blade Cuts

Ain't It Great to Be Dead?

When you die you think Heaven is waiting—
a light at the end of the tunnel;
a world where your soul is surrounded by beauty;
white light, puffy clouds, virgin angels.

There is a light at the end,
though it leads to darkness.
An icy blue tone it shines,
leading the dead as they walk through shadows.

Your body gets buried deep into cold soil.
Worms and insects find their way in,
squirming their shitty diseased bodies,
spreading their slime on your flesh.

They lay eggs in your brain,
eating all your flesh away.

The look that defined you
now food for the ground insects.

A lover of the dead digs you up,
cracking open the wooden case.
Your corpse sodomized daily,
your body kept under a bed.

Warm lips explore your coldness.
Love you'll never feel—
a selfish love that serves only one.

Eric Kapitan

Your soul gets pushed into the darkest corner,
assaulted by unseen demons.
They murder you over and over,
cutting off body parts one by one,
laughing as they painfully grow back.

Your new lover cuts you to pieces,
tossing everything away but your head.
She keeps it in a large fish tank in the den.

Ain't it great to be dead?

As The Blade Cuts

March of the Bloody Dead

I stand on a hilltop in the night,
looking down at the bright little lights,
peaceful and calm.
Soon they'll run.

In my hand I raise the stone blade to the sky.
I place it to my throat.

The thin stone pierces through my flesh like butter.
Blood spills out.
I raise my head opening up the wound.

Like a stream, my blood floods up to the sky,
infecting the clouds and turning them red.
Light flashes, lighting up the world.

My blood rains down—
rooftops and windows covered.
It absorbs into the soil,
reaching the caskets of the dead.

They awake.
Their eyes enraged in red.
Smashing through their wooden caskets,
they plow through the dirt,
rise up into the world.

They form lines of five—
thousands and thousands.
Their veins filled with my blood.
They feed off my rage.

Eric Kapitan

Marching through the graveyard,
heading toward the peaceful town.

As The Blade Cuts

Halloween Night II: The Sacrifice

Orange candlelight flickers in the night,
circling around a flat stone.
Dead leaves cover the ground.
Moon lights the night.

Jack-o'-lanterns glow in windows.
Children flood the streets looking for tricks or treats.
Something sinister is about to begin on this Halloween night.

A small group gathers.
Their hot breath floats in the air.
A baby is laid on the flat stone as it softly cries.

They chant in excitement.
The leader in the middle lifts up her hood.
Painted up as a demonic skull,
she holds a long dagger,
an ancient-looking thing.
She raises it to the sky.
The moon shines off the rusty blade.

"On this night, when the dead are free to roam, we offer this life to you! We bathe in the blood of its innocence."

"For him!" they all chant at once.

The dagger plunges into the soft chest.
Not much force is needed.
Bright red slithers down each side of the stone.
They take turns licking the blood.

Eric Kapitan

"Another enchanting Halloween night,"
one of them cheerfully proclaims,
smiling as she licks blood from her wrinkled lips.

As The Blade Cuts

Frozen Flesh

The beast sinks its teeth in me,
tearing away a chunk of flesh.
My blood falls in the snow,
leaving a trail as I walk.
Finally, I collapse,
snowflakes falling on my face.

I awaken.
Frozen blood sticks to my lips.
The hair on my beard stiff.
Brain feels as if it's being torn apart.

I hold the sides of my head tightly.
Blood drizzles out my ears.
Bite wound fills with green pus.
It pulsates like a heart,
becoming its own entity.

White foam runs from my mouth.
Body thrashes in violent rage.
The veins in my forehead expand.
Their color turns dark purple.

I stand up on my two feet,
screaming out in violent rage,
running through the woods uncontrollably.
The trees spin in my head.

I spin around and around,
blood and saliva flying from my face.
My heart explodes in my chest as I fall to the ground.

Eric Kapitan

My body covered in snow.
My eyes wide open.
Skin a pale blue tint.
Flesh begins to slowly crackle.
Skull emerges from my face.
My torso pops through the frozen flesh,
followed by my arms and legs.

My skeletal structure rises from worn-out flesh.
Eyeballs still in the sockets.
Cold blood sticks to my bones as I run off in the night.

As The Blade Cuts

Foreign World

Running through the darkness.
Trees blocking the moonlight.
A bright light follows behind me,
shining through the dead branches.
So strong its heat penetrates my skin.

My muscles weaken, but I continue to run.
My stomach cramps.
My heart pounds.
Knees buckle.

I trip and fall face-first into a rock.
My nose is broken as I taste blood.

The light hovers above me.
I scream as the heat burns into my back.

Surrounded by black.
Unknown creatures lit by red light.
They surround a body that is foreign to them,
touching and probing it with their long, gray fingers.

One creature places its hands on the chest of the body.
It waves them around causing the chest to burst open.
One by one, each creature pulls out an organ,
studying it with tiny slit-like eyes.

One holds the heart.
It sniffs it and then takes a bite.
Blood drips down the creature's chin.
He looks to the others and nods.

Eric Kapitan

They tear the body apart like ravaging dogs.
They suck out the eyeballs,
eat the flesh from the bone,
drink the blood like warm milk.

The creatures speak to one another in their minds.
Wanting more of this unknown animal,
they make plans to return to that foreign world—
the world known as Earth.

As The Blade Cuts

Inner Demons

Needle pressed to the skin.
It slides inside.
Bright-green liquid enters the stream.
Eyes widen.
Numb flows through the body.
Vibrant colors of red fill the vision in the eyes.

Crash!

The door bursts open.
A red demon stands in the doorway.
It screams loudly, showing its large, green fangs.

More demons appear behind it.
Licking their lips with long reptile tongues,
they form a circle ready to attack.

Memory flash.
Shotgun under the bed.
With a quick hand, the gun's in possession.
The demons snarl as they get blasted away.

The light from the gun echoes throughout the room.
Green blood pours as the bullets tear apart their heads.

The blast causes the ears to ring.
The last demon falls down dead.
The carpet stained with demon blood.
Their bodies cover the floor.

The red vision goes away.
The drug exits the veins.

Eric Kapitan

The shotgun is gone,
replaced with a knife.
Hands covered in blood.
Dark red-stained carpet.
Hand imprints on the walls.
The demons' bodies gone,
replaced with loved ones'.

As The Blade Cuts

Vampires Are Monsters

The sun lowers as it lights the sky one last time,
swallowed by the night.

The beast awakens—
demon under angel skin.

He walks the night,
looking for the right one—
the best one to feed his hunger,
to quench his pain.

The white-skinned creature sneaks in an open window.
A red-haired woman lies in bed asleep.
He runs his long fingernail up and down her neck,
gently piercing the skin.
A drop of blood emerges as his cold eyes widen.

His face splits down the middle.
Fangs run along the corners of each side.
Looking like a Venus Flytrap,
the creature pierces her soft skin.

She awakens with an immediate scream.
As blood is sucked from the neck,
the life from her body fades.
Her skin turns gray and gradually peels away.
He leaves nothing but her bones.

There was no love story here,
no tale of a misunderstood soul.
Vampires are monsters—
nothing more.

Eric Kapitan

Creature in the Swamp

There is an unknown beast living in the swamps.
The body of a man,
face of a hideous beast,
covered in black slime.
Its eyes a mix of yellow and red.
Its mouth full of rotten sharp teeth.

It's not in the swamp.
Today it's somewhere else.

It watches closely.
The young woman dips her toes into the lake.
The cold water makes her quiver as she dives in.
Her body adjusts and relaxes as she explores the depths.

The beast is patient—
watching her slowly,
waiting for her to come to it.

Her face rises above water.
The warm sun shines on her beauty.
She runs her fingers through her hair.
Pulled down into the water,
never coming back up.

The beast returns to its home in the swamp.
Under the cloudy water lies the woman's body—
her eyes glassy and wide open,
expression frozen in terror.
The creature drinks from her breasts and eats her flesh.
Her stomach expands as little worms pierce through.
A new breed is about to begin.

As The Blade Cuts

Whore Killin' (Yeah, You Be Offended!)

John sped down the highway at high speed,
drunk and high on a Friday night.
Tonight he did his usual thing:
whore killin'.

John hated whores,
hated everything 'bout 'em—
the way they looked,
the way they smelled,
the way they tasted.
He just loved slittin' their fuckin' throats—
that be the only thing he did like about 'em.

John took a swig of his beer,
spottin' one of 'em on the side of the road.
He could always tell the whores from the regular ladies.

John pulls his truck over to the side of the road.
He motions for the soon-to-be-dead whore to come over.
They work out a deal, and she hops on in.

He parks in an empty parking lot and gets down to it.
Things were gettin' hot and heavy.
The little whore straddled his lap, ridin' him hard.

John places his mouth to her neck, bitin' down on the flesh.
She didn't seem to mind, which mightily surprised him.
He pulls out a long blade from his boot.

The little whore started shakin' and twitchin'.
At first John didn't pay no attention.
He noticed how hot her body seemed to be gettin'.

Eric Kapitan

John's eyes got as big as a deer's stuck in headlights.
He noticed the skin from her face meltin' away.
The neck of the whore tears open.
Blood flows from the wound.
John screams as the little whore's head falls off,
landin' on his lap.

Somethin' started pushin' through the stump
where the whore's head once sat.
Somethin' black and fuckin' slimy.
John's lip quivers as he sees it's a head.
Bug-like with big red eyes,
it stares at John for a second before openin' its mouth,
pushing John's head inside.

John's body convulses as a loud crunch sound is heard.
The creature tears John's head off and eats it.
Blood from John's headless body rises from the stump.

As The Blade Cuts

You Go When You Gotta Go

Rain pours down, creating tiny puddles.
The rest area appears dead.
Parking lot lights flicker.

A man runs through the rain holding his sides.
Pushing the bathroom door with his shoulder,
he stumbles into the dirty bathroom,
falling to the floor,
moaning in pain.

He gets up and rushes into one of the stalls.
Caked shit covers the toilet seat.
The man does not seem to mind.

He leans his head forward, gagging.
His stomach in knots.
He dry heaves a few times
before he pukes out a black substance.
It falls into the toilet, splashing up on the seat.

Something much bigger appears to be pushing itself out.
Its gray, rubbery material pokes out of the man's mouth.
After a few moments of intense pain,
this unknown thing works its way out.
Water splashes his face
as it plops into the toilet.

It's the size of a head of lettuce,
blackish gray and covered in veins.
It's pulsating quite a bit,
creating waves in the toilet water.

Eric Kapitan

The man looks in shock at this thing
that was inside of him.
Covered in slime, it continues to pulsate,
thrashing as if trying to get out.

Something begins piercing through.
Orange slime bleeds from the hole.

A long, skinny snake-like arm shoots up from the toilet,
wrapping itself around the man's face as he screams.
He's pulled into the toilet head-first,
gargling and screaming as his body thrashes.
After a few moments he lies lifeless.

His body falls from the toilet,
a bloody stump revealed.
A slimy red hand emerges from the toilet.
It grips the side as it pulls itself out.

As The Blade Cuts

When It Came

This was a nice little town before it came.
The kinda town where you could leave your door unlocked,
children played in the streets,
jumped in leaf piles on fall days,
women walked with their babies in the summer.

That all changed when it came.
No one knows where it came from.
Some say from hell,
others say it lived in the woods.

A beastly monster with pale-gray skin.
It had the blackest eyes you've ever seen.
It preyed upon the town like a brooding storm.
It first killed the men—
both adult and boy—
skinned them alive,
drained them of their blood.

It kept the women alive—
well, all but one,
pregnant with a baby boy.
The beast split open her stomach,
ripping the child out of her.
It ate the baby right then and there,
swallowed the soft bones.

It enslaved the women of the town,
tasting them all.

Eric Kapitan

Sending them out to bring back men—
men whom it killed and ate.
Growing bored of the women,
it killed them all.
Made one big flesh stew,
consumed it in one big gulp,
scattered bones all through the streets.
On to the next town it went.

As The Blade Cuts

The Cornfield

A bright-orange haze covers the sky.
The tall corn sways back and forth,
silhouetted in dark yellow.
The chirping of birds fills the air.

A young boy sits on the porch.
His parents scream and argue inside.
Tears flood his eyes as he looks to the cornfield.
A scarecrow hovers above the cornstalk,
straw sticking out of its sides,
white face with mouth and eyes crudely drawn on.

The boy stares at it intently,
so intense it burns.
The sound of a hand smacking a face is heard.

A man holding a half-empty bottle grabs him by the hair.
The boy cries as he's dragged into the house.
A crow lands on the scarecrow's head.
Lightning flashes as dark clouds invade the sky.

The wind builds to a dangerous level.
Howling echoes throughout the night.
Rain pours flooding the earth.
Window shutters slam back and forth.
Lightning flashes, revealing the scarecrow.
Its brown hat blows off its head.
Drawn-on eyes and mouth washed away.
Thunder crackles loudly shaking the earth.

The rain and hellish wind suddenly stop,
as if someone simply flipped a switch.

Eric Kapitan

A huge beam of lightning comes down from the sky,
electrifying the scarecrow.
Sparks fly as the straw body shakes.
It seeps deep into the scarecrow surrounding it.
The lightning fades, and the scarecrow engulfs in flames.

Morning comes.
The birds chirp peacefully.
A blood trail leads to the cornfield.
Body parts scattered throughout—
hands, feet, arms, legs.
The scarecrow is gone.
In its place sits a man's severed head.

As The Blade Cuts

The Modern Monster

There is a monster not many can see.
It lurks carefully.
Disguised as a man or woman,
a friendly face with good intention.
Make no mistake—
it's evil.

It's not under your child's bed
nor hidden in the closet.
It doesn't eat your children like a witch.
No gingerbread house exists.
It has no lair on a mountain or in a cave.

It hides in cyberspace,
chatting with your children;
listening to what they have to say;
learning their likes and dislikes;
pretending they're interested;
treating them nicely;
giving them false power.

It can pretend to be another child,
sometimes someone slightly older.
True intentions it hides.

It grooms your child carefully—
playing with their minds,
leading them in a web.

It wants to experience your child's flesh,
their gift of youth,
their innocence.

Eric Kapitan

Smash it to pieces.
This monster hides in the souls of many,
almost impossible to weed out.

It feeds off parents' mistakes.
It's out there now,
ready to feast.

As The Blade Cuts

His Body Still Moves

Long ago in a different world, a man lived—
a nice and gentle soul;
a doctor loved and trusted by all.

Below the surface of his smile, something dark laid.
You see, the doctor had a desire for something—
something he could not live without:
the taste of human flesh.

He never murdered anyone.
Murder was against the good doctor's ethics.
He fulfilled his desire very easily.

He was also an undertaker.
He prepared dead folks for burial.
However, the bodies never got buried.

In the evening he helped young women in trouble.
They never asked what he did with the fetuses.

Every good thing must soon end.
The townsfolk hunted him down,
hung him high from a tree.

The oddest thing happened:
he did not die.
He hung from that tree for days.
His heart still beat.

They cut him down,
drowned him in the river.
Water filled his lungs, but he continued to live.

Eric Kapitan

They thought he made a pact with the devil.
Condemned him to the hot flames.

Tied him down tightly.
Covered him in gasoline.
They lit the match and watched it spread.
His skin burned and melted from the bone.

The doctor screamed as his body lay in flames.
The fine people of the town were sure they got him this time.
Reduced to nothing but charred flesh,
somehow, though, he still lived.

Right then and there they cut out his heart,
chopped it into pieces.

But still, his body moved.
They say it was because he consumed human flesh,
taking the souls of those he ate.

They threw him in a wooden box.
Wrapped it tightly in chains.
Buried him deep in the ground.

Many years and decades have gone.
The good doctor still lies in the ground,
his body covered in maggots,
bones frail and moldy.
His body still moves.

As The Blade Cuts

The Chair

He walks down the hall in chains,
disgusted by the smell of shit.

They push him in the chair,
strap him down tightly.
His heart pounding in his throat.

The switch is flipped.
Current flows through his body.
He shakes and quivers, screaming loudly.
Shit and piss cooks; the smell travels.

The strength of the current is raised.
Blood squirts from the eyes.
Skin bubbles like boiling water,
detaching from the body,
falling to the floor in a gooey puddle.

His eyeballs explode into a mess of pus and blood.
The switch turns off.
His head falls forward,
blood running from his open mouth.

From the shadows a red-eyed rat scurries over,
licking the blood from the floor.

Eric Kapitan

Hunger and Sex

Brooding clouds give the day a white gloomy look.
Thick fog sits in the air surrounding the graves.
Flowers covering the stones rot away,
like the corpses below.

A dark-haired woman stands.
She looks down at a gravestone.
Her eyes bright blue, skin milky white.
She wears a black-and-red dress.
Flowers held tightly in her hands.

She kneels in front of the grave.
A soft tear slides down her cheek.
Gently, she arranges the flowers in front of the stone.

A hand smashes through the dirt,
skin mummified and gray.
She gasps for air as it grabs her throat.

The hand lets go of her, pushing her backward.
She falls into a gravestone from behind.
Her head smacks hard into the marble.
In a daze she leans her back up against the grave.

With blurry vision she watches.
The undead ghoul slowly rises from its grave.
It stands before her—once a man, now a rotted corpse.
His torso exposed,
eyeball hanging from the socket.
He stumbles toward her as she lies helpless.

As The Blade Cuts

Grabbing her, forcing her to the ground.
He tears off her clothes, exposing her naked body.
smiling with delight as maggots fall from his mouth.

Pushing her arms above her head, he thrusts inside her.
She cries and whimpers in defeat.
He bites into her neck, pulling flesh with his teeth.
Blood runs from his mouth as she screams.

He bites hard into her cheeks, eating the skin from her face.
He cusps his mouth over her eye,
sucking it out from the socket.

An undead man filled with hunger and lust.
Thrusting deeply one final time.
He cums inside and stumbles away.

Naked and half-eaten,
she coughs up blood like a fountain.
Her heart ends.
Minutes go by before she awakes.
Her mind gone.
No soul exists.
She wants only two things:
hunger and sex.

Eric Kapitan

The Officer

The officer watches them enter the chamber.
Looking at their dirty sad faces.
Seeing the tears in their eyes,
the suffering on their faces.
He enjoys it.

A fond memory with each face he sees.
The man he made eat his own shit and piss.
The woman he raped multiple times,
made her children watch.

She got pregnant a few times.
He ripped the babies from her.
Threw them in the air for target practice.

A bullet to their little heads.
It made them explode.
Images of the gore caused him to smile.

It was all part of a process—
a process he created,
a process he loved.

Now came his favorite part.
After all the hell he put them through,
his face would be the last they see.
The thought aroused him.

The chamber door closed tightly.
Locked in place,
he looked at them through the window.
Their frail, naked bodies shivering.

As The Blade Cuts

Women hugging and kissing their children.
Men broken down to tears.
This was their end, and they knew it.

The officer flipped the switch.
Green gas filled the room.
They all passed out dead.

He opened the chamber door,
let the air filter out before entering.
He walked around, admiring the chamber of death,
stroking himself while he looked.
Pleased with what he caused,
what he created.

Their bodies in a pile.
Skin yellow and frail.
In the corner up against the wall sits a body—
the body of a young girl,
no older than six.
Her fingers slowly begin to move.
Her eyelids twitch.

Her eyes shoot open—
a bright-green color.
She screams loudly.
Black sludge oozes from her mouth.

The officer jumps in a panic.
Quickly pulling out his pistol,
he blasts bullets into the girl's tiny body.
The bullets have no effect.

Eric Kapitan

She jumps on top of him,
pushing him into his pile of death,
biting off large chunks of his flesh.

The officer screams in pain.
More spring to life,
their green eyes glowing with rage.

The undead monsters tear at his flesh,
piercing holes in the skin.
They tear off his limbs.
Blood sprays from the wounds.
The head savagely torn off,
blood erupts from the stump.
It flows in the air,
covering the windows,
lighting the chamber in red.

They break through the door.
Their eyes glowing in the night.
They stumble to the building next door,
where the soldiers lie asleep.

As The Blade Cuts

The Night Rage Filled the Air

There once was a woman who jogged through the woods,
not aware of the danger that lurked:
three dirty old men lived off the land.

They ambushed her,
took her away.
They hadn't seen a woman in years.
Had their fun with her
over and over until she puked.

They hanged her from a rope and slit her throat.
Watched the blood pour in a bucket.
Skinned her alive before plucking out her eyes.
Made stew with her skin and brains.

Even with her being dead,
more fun was to be had.
Every one of them liked it that way.

She sunk to the bottom of the river.
The dirty old men went back to camp.

Wind blew slowly.
Anger and rage filled the air.
Dark clouds invaded the star-filled sky.

Her body sat at the bottom.
Fish picked off her carcass.

Lightning flashed.
It pierced through the water,
electrifying her heart.

Eric Kapitan

It glowed bright red.

Her body floated above the water.
The dirty old men laid asleep around the fire.

She stood before them.
The orange flame slightly lit her face.
Water ran from her eyeless sockets.

Morning hit.
Smoke from the fire floated toward the blue sky.
The dirty old men still laid there,
skinless and eyeless.
Their burned dicks hung above the campfire.

As The Blade Cuts

The Road

Two women drive along a dirt road,
lost and unaware.
If you're a woman of the right type,
if you find yourself on this road,
you're done.

The young ladies' car hits a pothole,
blowing out a back tire.
The two women look at the damage.
Someone is watching.

That's when Jim and Bob strike.
They approach the ladies,
offer to change the tire.
After a few moments of small talk,
SMACK! SMACK!

Jim knocks them out with a tire iron.

They have a house in the woods,
swastikas crudely drawn on the walls.
The women kept in the basement,
raped daily until they become pregnant—
used for breeding their master race.

Jim and Bob only like the pure.
They cut the heads off the rest,
feed the bodies to their dogs.

After months go by,
the women both die.
Jim and Bob stand over their unmarked graves.

Eric Kapitan

Jim looks at Bob and smiles,
his teeth yellow and rotten.

"We goin' back to the road!"

As The Blade Cuts

One for the Fire

Heavy snow covers the ground,
weighing down on tree branches.

Footsteps crunch,
following a blood trail,
tracking wounded prey.
Beams of flashlights pierce through snowflakes.
Laughter and war cries roar through the trees.
The scared victim hides.

Covered in blood.
Shaking uncontrollably.
A mixture of snow and blood cakes her hair.
She holds her stomach tightly.
Blood leaks from the wound.
Frozen tears cover her face.
The snapping of a twig.
Someone is close.
Their flashlight shines in the distance.
Boots stomp through the white powder.

A big brute of a man stands
next to the trees she hides behind.
Dressed in a black jacket, fur-trimmed hood covering his head.
Breath exits his mouth like smoke.
He looks around, taking a swig from his flask.

Yelling in the distance heard.
It grabs his attention, and he walks away.
Relief flows up and down her body.

Eric Kapitan

She smiles, still shook up.
From behind, a hand grabs her by the hair,
pulling her head back.
A blade is pushed into her chin and up through her mouth,
cutting the tongue in two.
Blood drains out of her mouth,
slowly dripping down her lips.
Knife quickly pulled out as she falls to the ground.
A splash of red splatters on the snow.

"Another one for the fire!"

As The Blade Cuts

The Door at the End of the Hall

Family pictures hang in the hall—
smiling, happy faces.
When nightfall hits,
the smiles fade in darkness.

Yellow light creeps out under the crack
from the door at the end of the hall.
Flashing when machine sounds are heard.
Screaming, crying, and laughing soon follow.
The laugh is evil,
enjoying the pain.

Snip, snip.
Scissors cutting through flesh.
Crying and screaming fade.
The laughter sinister.

The yellow light gradually fades.
Dark blood creeps through the crack like spilled milk.

The door at the end of the hall.
Don't ever go inside,
unless you want to die.

Eric Kapitan

The Horse

Night in the little girl's bedroom.
Moonlight shines through the window blinds.
Shadows cover the pink walls.

In the center, many toys and dolls.
A carousel horse spins inside a snow globe.

Soft music plays.
Moonlight bounces off falling flakes,
glistening around the white horse.

The little girl lies asleep in her bed,
hugging her brown bear tightly.
One eye missing from its face.
The little girl's body shakes.
She rocks her head back and forth,
trying to wake up,
her face crunched up in deep distress.

Drip, drip.

The girl continues to lash back and forth.

Drip, drip.

Two drops of blood fall on the horse.
Two more drops, followed by a storm.

The blood rains inside the globe.
The horse spins as the sweet music plays.
Blood floods at the bottom and begins to rise.
The sleeping girl lets out a cry.

As The Blade Cuts

Horse covered in dark red.
The globe halfway full as the music slows.
The horse spins slower as well.
Innocence drenched in blood.

The girl rises from her bed,
her eyes wide open.
The globe filled with dark red.

She screams as the globe explodes.
Glass and blood fall to the floor.
Light bounces off the shards of glass.

Tears of blood run down the girl's cheeks.
The soft music still plays.
The horse continues to spin.

Eric Kapitan

My Darling

Order a drink, my darling—
something heavy and sweet.
Go to the bathroom, my darling.
Leave your drink in the open.
I'll add my sweetness.

That's right, my darling.
Finish every last drop.
You don't taste the difference.

It's OK, my darling.
You're off balance and light-headed.
In my car you go.

Don't worry, my darling.
You won't remember a thing.

As The Blade Cuts

He Never Let Go

Two lovers locked away,
holding each other tightly,
dehydrated from the heat.

She cries in his arms.
His grip tightens.
He leans forward and softly kisses her forehead.
Her face lies against his chest,
hearing his rapid heartbeat.

She knows what's coming.
She's aware of the outcome.
She doesn't care.
In his arms she's safe.

He found what he was looking for.
His strength is diminished.
His will crushed.
Holding her in his arms is all that's left.

"I won't let go," he whispers to her softly,

"no matter what."

The door closes, covering them in darkness.

Sun rays burst into the room
as the door is slammed open.
The sounds of eating and sucking heard.
White maggots squirm,
blanketing their bodies.

Eric Kapitan

Their flesh rotted and fused together,
becoming one entity.

Maggots morph into flies
as others crawl out of their eyes.
Their youth is gone.
Nothing more than a pile of decayed flesh.
Two carcasses.

He kept his promise.
No matter what, he never let go.

As The Blade Cuts

Carla and Craig

Carla and Craig—
two lost souls,
unwanted and abused.

Carla grew up in a trailer,
raised by her father alone.
Raped and cut, days on end.
He shared her with his friends.

Craig was born from sin:
father and mother of the same blood.
Chased out of town by family.
His father taught him the way.

Carla was teased and bullied at school.
It all stopped when Craig came.
Instant attraction and love.

They grew close together,
never apart.

As their bond strengthened, so did desire.
Craig taught Carla the art of murder.

They practiced on small animals,
collecting the bones.

A special day came:
Carla's eighteenth birthday.
Craig drugged her father,
handed Carla the knife.

Eric Kapitan

Rage overflowing,
she pushed the knife deep inside.
Watched her father's blood spill.

She smiled as red covered her hands.
Craig knew she wasn't done.

She slid off his pants and cut off his cock—
the cock he made her suck,
the cock he forced inside.
She shoved it deep in his mouth.

They traveled the world.
Covering the road in blood and guts.

Raping.
Murdering.
Their blood lust never cleansed.

They drank too much.
Snorted some bad coke.
Their car steered off the road.

Craig died instantly.
Carla died slowly.

Their souls fell to the depths of hell.
Flesh ripped apart,
torn from the bones.

They wandered the abyss for decades.
Finally finding each other again,
they embrace in a deep kiss.
Their bodies engulf in flames.

As The Blade Cuts

Blood Red

Trapped in darkness,
walking mindlessly.
A small twinkle of light appears.
It grows wider as it becomes stronger.
Eyes blink as the light burns bright.
Feeling the warmth the closer it gets.

The white submerges around the black,
eating up the darkness.

Twenty-one naked virgins stand in a circle,
their skin milky and smooth.
Long, silky, and shiny hair flow beautifully.
Their expressions filled with enticement.

Slowly their skin fades to gray.
Maggots slither from their nostrils.
Their teeth fade into black as they fall out.

Blood pours from their eyes.
Clumps of hair pulled out.
One by one they melt into a pile of flesh.

The white light turns blood red.
Maggot eggs hatch from the dead skin.
Insects swarm the paradise.

Eric Kapitan

Today Is My Day

Loud piercing sound of my alarm echoes.
My tired eyes open.
I collect my thoughts for a moment.
Today is the day.

I pull off the blankets and jump out of bed.
My bare feet run across cold floor.

Back tingles.
Warm water runs down my body.
My thoughts quickly race.
Today is the day.
Today is my day.

I look at myself in the mirror.
Put on my blue tie.
I admire how it looks with my black shirt.
I pick my glasses up off the nightstand.
Clean them thoroughly,
not leaving a speck of dirt.

I eat a big breakfast.
Go to the closet and grab my things.

On any other day I'm a loser,
just another asshole.
I walk through crowds unnoticed.
No one cares to know my name.

That all changes today.

As The Blade Cuts

They will speak my name.
They will talk about my past,
who I am,
what I did.

In this world,
you gotta think big.
Hard work won't get you attention,
neither will talent.

I pull the gun out of my closet,
load it, and put it inside my jacket.

I will bathe in strangers' blood for attention.
Their lives will be sacrificed for my fame.
They won't be remembered.
Their faces will fade.
Their deaths become a number.
I will be the one that's known.

My face will be remembered forever.
My crime glorified.
They will question why I did it.
My family will be blamed,
so will music and movies.

I'll become a celebrity,
a martyr for my fame.

Walk out the door with gun raised.
I shoot my first bullet toward fame.

Eric Kapitan

The Collection

I lock the door to my room.
Wife's gone.
Now is the time.

I open up the closet,
taking out the board from the back wall—
my treasures hidden behind.

I smile as I look at them all.
My heart warms and tingles.

A hair tie.
A bracelet.
A purse.
Each tells a story.
Remembering everything about their owners.
The way they looked.
Smelled.
The last expression on their faces.

I pick up the hair tie, put it to my nose.
The smell of her still lingers.
Her beautiful face flashes in my brain.
Angela was her name.
She was walking home from school.
She didn't make it there.

I work with her father.
He talks to me often.
If only he knew.

As The Blade Cuts

Then there was Amy.
Her sneaker I kept after I cut off her foot.
Specks of blood remain on the white laces.

These objects bring me pleasure—
remind me of good memories.
Memories only do it for me for so long.

The itch is back.
The need.
The want.
I'll be adding more to the collection.

Eric Kapitan

Perfection

The perfect one is out there.
I see them every day,
in different pieces.

They exist in many.
I saw their eyes on Thursday,
their hair on Friday.
Her legs on Monday.
When I see a piece, I take a picture.

I clear off my kitchen table.
Place each picture in a row.
Stare at them intently.
Cut out each piece I like from the photos.
Paste my perfect mate together.

At night I track them down.
Hacking each piece away.
The red makes me sick.
Can't stop until I have each one.

It's the end of the week.
All the pieces together,
locked away in a downstairs freezer.

I work into the night,
sewing each piece elegantly together.
I glue in the eyes,
a perfect shade of blue.

My work is done.
My beautiful angel.

As The Blade Cuts

The cure to my disease.
My loneliness.

I talk to her all night,
share with her my darkest secrets,
my biggest fears.

Each victim came with baggage,
imperfections, and annoying habits.
She has none of that nonsense.
She lives for me.
She lives because of me.

Each piece of her is perfection.

Eric Kapitan

Food for the Maggots

Dark blue sits above the world.
Sun lights it up.
Paved road absorbs heat,
making it hot to the touch.

A thin trickle of red runs down the middle.
The longer the line goes, the thicker and messier it gets.
At the carcass of a dead dog it ends—
a big golden retriever.

The body convoluted and twisted,
bone sticking out the end of the front leg.
Brain matter falls out the side of the head.
The tongue hangs out, cooked on the pavement.
Dark blood stains cover the once-beautiful coat.

Buzzing is heard as the wind gently blows.
Growing louder and louder.
Getting closer.
A fly lands on the dead dog's eye,
its body a shiny green color,
eyes big and bright red.
Crawling around the carcass in excitement.
Trying to find the best spot.

More buzzing is heard as more flies emerge,
circling the corpse as if guarding it.

The dog slowly rots away.
Tiny eggs hatch into white wormed larva.
Their bodies squirm and feed into the stinking corpse.
More eggs hatch as the flesh collapses within itself.

As The Blade Cuts

A suckling sound heard.
Hundreds of maggots surround the body,
piling up onto one another.
The poor pup's body vanishes,
a sea of crawling white.
Food for the maggots.

Eric Kapitan

Feast for the Crabs

Falling through pure darkness,
arms and legs shaking.
Body smashes into the sea.

Water rushes to the brain.
Clothes stick to skin.
Eyes widen.
Breath held tightly.

The body thrashes trying to reach the top.
Ice-cold water pours through the lungs.
Mind racing in delirium.
Thought process impossible.

Body shakes without control until movement slows.
The head leans forward.
Lifeless, the corpse floats to the top.

The sun slowly rises from slumber.
The sound of waves and wind mix together.
A dead man washes up on shore.

His skin pale and blue,
clothes torn apart.
A crab crawls from the wide-open mouth.
More and more crabs appear, both small and large.
They feast on the cold, dead flesh.

Children rush the beach with surfboards in hand.

As The Blade Cuts

Heat Wave

In a small town the heat climbs
from bearable to horrible,
reaching a whopping hundred and five degrees.

The humidity rises with the heat.
People vomit in the streets.
Electricity gets fried.
Air conditioning dies out.
Food goes bad.

Slowly the madness descends.
Sweat drips from faces.
The heat seeps in their brains.

Simple disagreements turn to arguments.
They lash out like deranged beasts.
Places are looted.
People killed and injured.

A young woman assaulted by four men.
Right there in the middle of the sidewalk,
crowds look on.

Bodies lie scattered in piles.
Swarms of black flies hover above them.
A man on fire frantically runs down the street.

Police try and take control.
The town overpowers them.
Placing their dirty fingers in their eyes,
squishing them like grapes,
they eat the skin from their bones.

Eric Kapitan

Clouds darken the sky.
Water drips down slowly.
After a few moments it begins to pour.

A naked man throws a woman to the ground.
Savagely tearing off her clothes,
he spreads her legs wide,
forcing himself inside.
He looks up with his mouth wide.
Cold rain runs down his throat.
He screams wildly.

The heat wave continues.

As The Blade Cuts

Blood Flow

Bare feet stand on cold stone.
Looking up at the heavens.

Body exposed and naked.
Mouth opens wide.
Blood rains from the sky.
Dark red flows over old skin.
The taste of iron sits on the tip of the tongue.

It pours down the throat.
Being recharged.
Building strength.

Thousands of unwanted babies from above.
Masked butcher cuts their throats, letting the blood flow.
Restoring the youth of the old.

Eric Kapitan

Home Invasion

The family prays over dinner.
Their windows and doors smash open.
Four men dressed in black enter.

They beat up the father and son,
threaten the mother and daughter,
bring them to the living room.

The daughter screams as her breasts are fondled.
They promise they won't hurt them.
Money is their demand.

The father gives them the combination,
crying as he hands over their belongings.

They shoot the father in the head,
break the son's neck,

take turns with the mother and daughter,
carving names in their flesh.

Behind the house a bonfire burns high.
The flames burn like the ones in hell.
Piled in the flames lie the bodies.

Mother and daughter on top,
father and son below.
Their flesh turns black.

The four men sit at the dinner table,
smacking their lips together like slobs,
eating the meal the family prayed over.

As The Blade Cuts

Dinnertime

Water and blood mix together,
circling down the drain.
I turn off the faucet,
dry my hands.
They remain stained.

I look over at the counter.
Your tongue sits on a plate.
That tongue covered my skin hours earlier.
It pleasured me.
Now it's going to pleasure again.

I light up the stove,
place a black pan on top.
The flame circles in a blue and purple color.
Once full circle, it turns a bright orange.

I watch butter melt away.
I look at the tongue for a bit before gently putting it in.
It sizzles and smokes upon touching the hot surface.
I let it brown on each side.

Cartoons play loudly on the TV.
Your body sits in front of it.
That's funny to me.
Your skin is a bluish white.
The life is gone from your eyes.

Your teeth removed—
I plucked them out for my comfort.
Your mouth surrounded in bloodstain,
like badly applied lipstick.

Eric Kapitan

I set the table and light candles,
pour myself a dark beer.
It really browned nicely.
My knife slices into it.
I feel the juices.
Stick my fork inside,
take a big bite.
It's an explosion of flavor.
What part shall I try next?

As The Blade Cuts

The Blackest Day

After we feast, the clouds circle the sky.
I know what's coming:
the darkest day there is.

On this day people go mad.
They swarm like locusts.
Determined, they plow over anything and everyone
just to get what they want—
material things.

The doors open.
They sheepishly run in,
consuming everything in sight,
arguing like lions fighting over meat.

Circling around me,
rage in their eyes.
"Where is this?"
"Where is that?"
"Why don't you have this?"
"I want this now!"

They grow angrier.
Their demands unmet.
Sweat pours down my forehead.
Growing light-headed.
My eyes burn from the flickering light.
The pain in my head grows deeper.
Their voices flood my ears.

Eric Kapitan

They point at me in anger.
Bad breath and horrible body odor flood my nose,
entering my mouth.
I gag as my stomach grows weak.

I swallow back the vomit.
My face deep red.
Eyes squint in rage.

Light glows on a chainsaw sitting on a shelf.
I pick it up and rev it.

The angry mob slowly steps back.
I run at them, sawing into their flesh as my laugh echoes.

A middle-aged woman's severed head flies in the air.
Blood floods in the aisles.
It splatters on the toys and electronics they desired.

A sea of blood streams behind those who rush to the exits.
The doors close before they can leave.
I ride in on the blood wave and splatter their brains.

I continue my quest until the mass consumerism is dead.
Their bodies and limbs pile high to the ceiling.
I stand on top of it all,
swinging my bloody chainsaw,
covered head to toe in the blood of shoppers.
The white of my smile clashes against the red.

The darkest of all days.
The blackest of all Fridays.
They shopped, and I chopped.
Black Friday is dead.

As The Blade Cuts

Merry Fucking Christmas

A blanket of snow covers the ground.
Moonlight casts it in blue tint.
Huge snowflakes fall, adding to the pile.

Houses covered in lights flood the neighborhood.
A wreath hung on every door.

In a church they sing Christmas songs,
dressed in white, holding candles.

Warm flames burn in the fireplace.
The fire crackles and pops warming the house.
Three bright-red stockings hang above.

A Christmas tree sits in the corner
stuffed with presents below.
Beautiful mixtures of color wrap the green tree.
The smell of pine floods the room.

A fabulous feast sat at the table:
homemade stuffing,
creamy mashed potatoes,
stuffed mushrooms with a hint of garlic,
a big juicy turkey carved up, ready to go.

The family sits around the table on this magical Christmas Eve,
covered in blood,
throats slashed,
the electric turkey carver stuck in Dad's head.
Pieces of skull and brain peak out from behind the blade.

Eric Kapitan

Little Timmy won't get his train set.
Mom won't get that diamond.
No new fishing pole for good old dad.

Covered in blood, a man sits in the den.
Lighting up a cigarette, he walks into the kitchen,
picking up Dad's half-drunk beer.
He guzzles it down.

Noticing the striking beauty of Mom,
he softly strokes her bloody face.
Lifting her up over his shoulder,
upstairs they go.

Merry fucking Christmas.

Please don't close this book just yet!

Thank you for purchasing and reading this book. Please feel free to write a review on the books amazon page:

http://amzn.com/1519198728

Other Books Written by Eric Kapitan

Darkness: Poems of Extreme Horror
(available in both paperback and Kindle format)
http://amzn.com/1516824822

Stay Connected with Eric Kapitan

Facebook
https://www.facebook.com/eric.kapitan

Twitter
https://twitter.com/eric_kapitan

Amazon Author Page
http://www.amazon.com/author/eric.k

About the Author

Eric Kapitan has a huge admiration for all things horror. He loves to tell stories that can both disturb and entertain a reader. His favorite horror film series is *Phantasm*. His favorite book is *The Bighead* by Edward Lee.

Eric currently lives in a small town in Vermont where he also grew up. He enjoys spending time with friends and family as well as drinking a nice, cold Vermont-brewed beer.

Made in the USA
Columbia, SC
12 May 2023